NO.1 BOY DETECTIVE

Gruesome Ghosts

Collect all the No. 1 Boy Detective books!

NO.1 BOY DETECTIVE

Gruesome Ghosts

Barbara Mitchelhill
Illustrated by
Tony Ross

Andersen Press • London

For Charlotte, Thomas and James with love

This edition first published in 2017 by
Andersen Press Limited
20 Vauxhall Bridge Road
London SW1V 2SA
www.andersenpress.co.uk

First published by Andersen Press Limited in 2009

2 4 6 8 10 9 7 5 3

British Library Cataloguing in Publication Data available.

ISBN 978 1 78344 669 8

Printed and bound in Great Britain by Clays Ltd, Elcograf S.p.A.

Chapter 1

Even though I'm famous for my brilliant detective work, I had never had to solve a ghost crime. Kidnappings, yes. Robberies, yes. But last week, I took on the Case of the Gruesome Ghosts and this turned out to be the most spooky and dangerous case EVER.

It started like this. We had a new girl in our school called Annabelle Harrington-Smythe. She was a year older than me and had great big blue eyes and long blonde hair. I noted these facts in my detective's notebook and did a drawing for my records.

Last Wednesday, I was in the playground when I noticed her sitting on a bench with Dixie Stanton (who is a real pain). I was near enough to hear what they were saying.

'It's terrible,' said Annabelle. 'My grandparents have ghosts in their house.'

'Cool!' said Dixie Stanton.

'No. Not cool,' said Annabelle, biting on her lower lip. 'There are noises and everything. I can't stay there any more. It's too scary.'

It was clear to me that she was worried, so I stepped forward. 'You sound as if you could do with my help.'

She looked up at me and frowned. I was a bit miffed when she said, 'What can you do? You're just a kid.'

Obviously, being new to the area, she hadn't heard of my reputation as a detective.

'I may be a kid,' I replied, 'but I have a supersonic brain.'

All she said was 'Really?' Then she walked off with Dixie Stanton, giggling. That's girls for you.

I didn't let it bother me, though. I was determined to show her how brilliant I was by solving her grandparents' ghost problem.

This is how I did it.

First, I called a meeting of my trainee detectives who are mostly in my class (except Lavender who is only six). I told them my plan.

'Before we can do anything,' I explained, 'I have to get the facts. So I'll go to see Annabelle's grandparents and discuss the problem.'

Tod, who often asks difficult questions, said, 'Why would they talk to you, Damian? You're not a grown-up, are you?'

'Simple,' I said. 'I'll dress up as a reporter. I'll say I'm doing an article for the paper. They'll talk to me then, won't they?'

Winston stood with his arms folded and shook his head. 'You're a bit small for a reporter,' he said, rather hurtfully, I thought.

'I can make myself taller,' I replied.

'Impossible,' said Tod.

I was beginning to lose my patience. 'Listen, I can make myself taller with Mum's high-heeled boots. But I'll need a pair of long jeans to cover them.'

Harry Houseman, the tallest boy in our class, was the obvious choice.

'How about lending me yours, Harry?'

He stood looking at me, thinking (which takes Harry quite a long time). Eventually he said, 'You can borrow my jeans if I can be on the ghost case with you. I've never seen a ghost.'

I wasn't sure. I usually work alone on difficult cases.

But Harry was keen.

'If you let me,' he said, 'you can have my dad's black coat as well. That'll make you look like a real reporter.'

How could I refuse? With high-heeled boots, long jeans and a black coat it was a perfect

disguise. All I needed was a false moustache. Luckily I had already made one from brown wool I found in Mum's work box.

'OK, Harry,' I said, slapping him on the shoulder. 'It's a deal. You can come on the case.'

He was dead excited. 'I'll bring my camera,' he said. 'I can be the photographer.'

It wasn't a bad idea. Harry looked like an adult. After all, he was as tall as Mr Grimethorpe, our teacher.

We planned to call on Annabelle's grandparents the next day, after school. Once I'd solved this case, Annabelle would take me seriously and treat me with respect.

Chapter 2

On Thursday morning, I stuffed my disguise into my sports bag and told Mum I'd be late home.

'Football practice,' I said. (I don't like telling lies but sometimes they are necessary in my line of work.)

After school, Harry and I got changed in the cloakroom ready to walk to Annabelle's grandparents' house*. It wasn't far away but it took ages because of Mum's high-heeled boots. Walking was IMPOSSIBLE. My toes were scrunched up into the pointy toes and I wobbled so much that I fell over twice. In the end, I had to hang onto Harry.

Annabelle's grandparents lived at the Grange, which was a huge house in Rigby Road. It had a massive garden and great big iron gates at the front.

---

*I got their address from Annabelle's friend (Lulu Butterworth) who agreed to tell me if I stopped pestering her.

'They must be dead rich,' said Harry. I pushed the gates open and we made our way to the front door and knocked. After waiting forever, an old lady came and opened it. I knew it must be Annabelle's grandma – even though she was very old and wrinkly and wearing pink fluffy slippers.

'Yes?' she said, staring right at us and squeezing her eyes on account of her bad eyesight.

'I'm a reporter from the Evening Post,' I said. (This was another necessary lie.) 'I wonder if I could ask you a few questions.'

She looked puzzled. Harry waved his camera in the air and grinned at her. 'I'm the photographer,' he said, which seemed to make her even more confused.

'I think you'd better come in,' she said, turning away and shuffling down the hall. 'My husband will talk to you, I'm sure.'

Major Harrington-Smythe (Annabelle's grandad) was sitting in a chair by the fire reading the paper.

'These young men are reporters, dear,' his wife said.

The Major folded his paper, looked up and stared. 'Reporters, eh? Well, well, well. I know that policemen look younger these days – but now reporters are looking like schoolboys.' He threw his head back and laughed and I noticed he had a set of perfect teeth like Annabelle. But were they real?

'I'm here to write an article,' I said, pulling out my notebook and waving my pencil. 'I've come about the ghosts.'

At the word 'ghosts', Mrs Harrington-Smythe gave a gasp and began to tremble. She was obviously SCARED STIFF.

The Major frowned and leaned forward confidentially.

'I'm afraid my wife is very nervous,' he said. 'It's all because of the noises in the night. You may think this is ridiculous . . . but we've seen things, too.'

'Seen things? You mean ghosts?'

'In fifty years nothing like this has ever happened,' said Annabelle's grandad. 'I don't believe in ghosts myself.'

This was getting dead interesting and I was writing loads of notes.

'Two months ago,' the Major continued, 'a historian came to see us. He was researching my great, great grandfather, Bartholomew Harrington-Smythe.'

He turned and pointed to a large painting on the wall. It was of a man with a top hat and a white beard. Very impressive.

'When this man told us that Bartholomew was a murderer . . . Well, we were shocked, weren't we, dear?'

'Shocked!' Mrs Harrington-Smythe replied. 'Shocked something shocking.'

The Major continued. 'He said Bartholomew had killed a young woman in the next village. Terrible. Terrible.'

He wiped his forehead with his handkerchief.

'Soon after we'd learned all this,' his wife said, wiping her nose, 'I saw the ghosts for the first time.'

I scribbled notes as fast as I could. 'How often do they come?' I asked.

Mrs Harrington-Smythe began to sob. 'The poor woman comes every night,' the Major replied, 'screaming and pacing the floor. It's a gruesome sight. I can't stand it. We'll have to sell the house.'

There was a pause as the two old people looked at me, their faces grey with worry.

'Have no fears,' I said. 'I am here to help.'

I stood up and revealed my identity.

I flung off my coat.

I removed my shades.

I ripped off my false moustache.

'I have deceived you,' I said. 'I am not a reporter at all. I am Damian Drooth, famous boy detective, and I have come to get rid of these terrible ghosts.'

The Major's mouth fell open.

'Damian Drooth? Boy genius?' he said. 'I've read about you in the paper. I'm so grateful that you've come.'

'Grateful, grateful,' said Mrs Harrington-Smythe, smiling broadly.

(I noticed she had only one or two teeth but they were real, unlike her husband's.)

I already had a plan worked out and, after Annabelle's grandma had fetched us some orange juice and two plates of cakes, I explained it all.

'I will come and spend Saturday night in the house,' I said.

Harry dug me in the ribs. 'Don't forget me. You promised.'

I took another slice of chocolate cake.

'But won't you be terrified?' asked Mrs Harrington-Smythe.

I shook my head. 'A detective only looks at the facts. First I need to do some research.'

We made time for a jam doughnut and then we left the Grange, promising we would be back in two days' time.

Chapter 3

The following day, I called a meeting of my trainee detectives in the playground. Winston, Harry, Tod and his sister, Lavender (who is only six).

'I don't know much about ghosts,' I said. 'So I need to find out about 'em. We'll go down to the library after school and do some serious research. OK?'

They were all very keen.

That afternoon, we met outside the library. Tod and Lavender brought Curly, who is a very intelligent dog and part of our Detective School.

'I bet Miss Travis will be pleased to see us,' I said. (Miss Travis was the town's librarian and we hadn't seen her for ages.)

She was there behind the desk when we walked in and I thought she looked rather nervous.

'Damian!' she said. 'I see you've brought your friends with you.'

'Yes,' I replied. 'We're doing research.'

'Research?' she said as if she didn't know what it meant.

'Research into ghosts,' I said as we set off towards the shelf with books beginning with G.

But Miss Travis shouted, 'Damian! Please go and wipe your feet. Now!' (If you ask me, she should read the notices in the library.)

PLEASE BE QUIET AS PEOPLE MAY BE READING

Just to please her, we all trooped back into the lobby and very carefully wiped the mud off our shoes. But was that enough? No!

'And take your dog outside,' she said, pointing to Curly. 'They are not allowed in the library.'

Tod was shocked. 'But it's cold outside,' he said. 'She could get pneumonia.'

'Yeth,' said Lavender. 'Thee might die.'

'Shame,' said Winston.

I leaned over Miss Travis's desk and mentioned, ever so quietly, that dogs had rights the same as humans.

'Not in my library they don't,' Miss Travis shrieked in a very un-librarian way.

Then Lavender
burst into tears
at the thought
of her precious
dog being left
tied to a drain pipe.

'Thee's going to die,' she hollered
and the other kids joined in a protest.

'It's not right.'

'You wouldn't like to be left outside.'

'Dogs have feelings, too, you know.'

A queue of people was forming as
they waited to check out their books
and they weren't very pleased. They
were probably dog lovers. Miss Travis
was in a bit of a panic and looked
flushed.

'No worries, Miss Travis,' I said.
'Curly is very well behaved. You carry
on with your work and I'll do mine.'

We turned and walked towards the

non-fiction section where we carefully tied Curly to the leg of a chair.

There were loads of books on ghosts so we spread them out across two tables.

'Oi!' said a man in a woolly hat. 'Are you taking over the whole library?'

'We're doing police work*,' I explained. 'If I were you, I'd go and sit over in the children's section. It's really quiet there.'

His mouth fell open. I guess he was shocked to learn that someone as young as me was working for the police force.

We spent a long time (at least fifteen minutes) looking through the books.

---

*This was a lie number 3 but, as I said to Harry, if the police were doing their job properly, I wouldn't have to sort out people's problems.

In the end, this is what we found out:

Some people don't believe in ghosts.
Ghosts walk through walls.
Ghosts are unhappy 'cos they've probably murdered somebody.

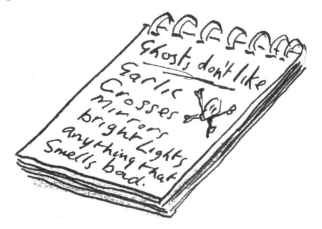

By the time I'd written masses of notes, the rest of the gang were getting bored. Lavender was playing Hide and Seek with Harry around the bookshelves. Winston and Tod were kicking a ball of paper across the floor.

Even the dog was
whining. I don't
blame them.
It's hard work
doing research.

'Right,' I
said when I'd
finished. 'Let's go.'

We were just walking
out through the door when Miss Travis,
who had been very busy stamping
books and stuff, called out, 'Damian!'
and waved her hand in the air.

I waved back. ''Bye, Miss Travis.'

She waved more frantically. 'What
about all the books you left on the
table?'

'Thanks, Miss Travis,' I said. 'They
were very useful.'

It always pays to be polite.

Chapter 4

This was my plan for getting rid of the gruesome ghosts:

I would tell Mum I was having a sleepover at Harry's house. Harry would tell his mum he was coming to mine.

It was a brilliant idea.

'That's a brilliant idea,' said Harry.

And when I told Mum about the sleepover, she seemed really pleased. It turned out she was having some friends in for a meal that night.

'That's a brilliant idea,' she said (which is just what Harry said).

'Glad you think so, Mum,' I replied.

'Well, you do have a habit of upsetting things when I've got people round, Damian.'

Cheek! Some mothers can be so critical.

On Saturday morning, I spent time gathering the things on my list. These were:

1. Garlic.

There were two bulbs of garlic in the fridge but that wasn't enough so I took the onions in the pantry as well. Still not enough, so I dug up the leeks in the garden. Leeks are very like onions which are very like garlic so I guessed they would do. I planned to make a circle around the house in the hope of frightening the spooks.

2. Wooden cross

Harry was making a wooden cross as his dad had loads of wood in the shed. He is dead good at woodwork.

3. Mirror

Lavender brought a mirror from her bedroom but it was useless. It was pink and had 'My little princess' written on the frame in diamonds. There was no way I was taking that to the Grange. Instead, I went into Mum's bedroom and unhooked the mirror off the wall. It was bad luck that it slipped. But, it didn't smash. There was only a crack which Mum would never notice.

By five o' clock, I'd packed my bag and added a few delicious snacks from the fridge, as I believe that ghost watching can make you quite hungry.

Mum came with me to the front door. 'I want you to be on your very best behaviour when you're at Harry's house,' she said, thinking I was going for a sleepover.

26

She went on about brushing my teeth, remembering my manners, not burping at the table, not picking my nose or arguing at bedtime. I bet Harry didn't have to go through all this. He had sensible parents.

Once I'd left our house, I walked round to the Grange where the team were waiting by the gates.

'Right,' I said, opening my sports bag. 'Surround the house with this lot.' And I tipped out the garlic, the onions and the leeks.

'Do you think it'll work?' Harry asked.

'Dunno,' I said. 'We'll just try everything.'

We did our best but there wasn't enough to go round the house. Instead, we made a big pile in front of the door – which was the next best thing.

Then the gang went home, leaving Harry and me to do the real work.

Inside the Grange, there was a fantastic tea waiting for us in the kitchen. Mrs Harrington-Smythe had cooked toad-in-the-hole, mashed potatoes and peas, with apple pie and ice cream for afters. It was delicious. I was so full that I went off the idea of ghost hunting.

I fancied putting my feet up and watching the telly. But no. A detective never sleeps. I had work to do.

'Where are we going to spend the night?' I asked as the Major opened a small box of chocolates.

'The ghosts appear in our bedroom,' he said, passing the box to Harry. 'I expect you'll want to keep a watch from there?'

'Oh my goodness,' said Mrs Harrington- Smythe. 'Such young boys. So brave. Won't you be terrified?'

'I'm cool,' I said. 'I've faced serious criminals before now. A couple of ghosts aren't going to scare me off.'

'Nor me,' said Harry, helping himself to the only Fudge Fancy (I was not pleased as this is my favourite).

'OK then,' said the Major, 'I'll take you upstairs.'

Chapter 5

The house was like Dracula's castle – dark and very spooky. As we followed the Major slowly up the stairs, every step creaked. **CREEEAAKKK!**

I noticed other creaks, too.

CREEEAAKKK! CREEEAAKKK! CREEEAAKKK!

But these turned out to be the Major's knees which were old and knobbly and very noisy.

At the top of the stairs, was a corridor that smelled of damp and was lit by one measly light bulb.

It was freezing cold and there wasn't even a carpet on the floor. I couldn't understand why two old people wanted to live in place like that. In my opinion, they needed a nice bungalow with plastic windows, central heating and a telly in every room.

The Major stopped outside a large oak door. 'This is our bedroom,' he said. 'I hope you'll be comfortable.'

He opened the door which – like the stairs and the Major's knees – creaked very loudly. **C R E E E A A K K K !**

'Candles are by the bedside,' he said. 'Just in case you need them. We've been having a lot of power cuts lately.'

You should have seen the bedroom. It was massive – about twenty times the size of mine at home – but there were wood panels on the walls instead of some nice wallpaper. Maybe they couldn't afford it.

There was one of those four-poster beds they have in horror movies with curtains round them. When the Major had gone, Harry leapt onto it and started using it like a trampoline.

'It's brilliant,' said Harry, doing a double twist. 'But you'd think they'd have a TV in here, wouldn't you? I'm missing Dr Who.' He did a triple flip and sank onto the mattress. 'Don't suppose you've got anything to eat, have you, Damian?'

I was feeling a bit peckish myself as it was at least half an hour since we finished our tea. 'Fancy this?' I said

and pulled out a packet of tortilla chips
from my bag. They were in a big packet
– very fancy – but they looked like
triangular crisps to me.
I'd found them in the
kitchen with a couple of
tubs of dip-thingies.

'Anything else?'

I took out two huge slices of
strawberry meringue which I had found
in the fridge. It looked really good.

'We should have a midnight feast,'
said Harry.

But we decided we couldn't wait
that long. So we spread the food out
on the bed like a picnic and helped
ourselves. (Very good – except for the
dip thingies which had bits in them and
were disgusting.)

It was some time later that I realised
I needed to go to the loo.

Bravely, I stepped out into the spooky corridor and walked down, opening all the doors, but I couldn't find a bathroom.

I was at the far end, when the bulb dangling from the ceiling began to flicker. Flicker, flicker, flicker. Then it went out.

Suddenly, I was alone in the pitch dark. What should I do?

With my heart pounding, I put my hands flat on the wall and tried to feel my way back to the bedroom. But before I had taken more than a few steps, I heard a terrible noise.

'oooooooooooooooOH!'

I stood frozen to the spot with my knees knocking like the maracas in the school band.

It was then that a figure appeared

in the dark, glowing a ghostly white. It was moving slowly towards me and behind was a smaller shape, misty and almost invisible.

I had never seen a ghost before. Now I was face to face with two of them, I did the only thing I could think of.

I screamed.

'Aaaaaaaaaaaaaaaaaaagh!'

I fled back along the corridor, barged into the bedroom and slammed the door behind me.

Harry was sitting on the edge of the bed, lighting a candle.

'We've had a power cut,' he said.

'The ghosts have turned it off,' I yelled. 'They're in control. They're in the corridor.'

'What are you on about, Damian?' asked Harry, putting a lit candle on the bedside table.

'Ghosts!' I said. 'I've seen 'em. Help me move this chest of drawers across the door. We've got to keep them out.'

Harry's brain might be slow but he is very strong. Together we pushed the chest across the room. We heaved and we shoved until it blocked the door.

But when we'd finished, Harry said, 'What's the point of that. Spooks can walk through walls, can't they?'

It's not often Harry is right. But that time he was. Nowhere was safe. We were in deadly danger.

Chapter 6

As the head of a famous detective school, I had to set a good example and hide my fear from Harry. And when the noise came again –

HOOOOOOOOOOOOOOO!

– I leapt onto the bed, grabbing the wooden cross, and holding it at arm's length in front of me.

'You don't frighten me,' I called out towards the door. 'I have the tools to finish you off.'

This was bold talk which I hoped would scare the spectres away.

But the noise came again.

'WAAAAAaaaaaaa.'

My stomach began to churn like chocolate in a chocolate factory. How long had we got before the gruesome ghosts appeared in the bedroom?

I must admit, Harry didn't seem bothered. He was pressing his ear against the door.

'Listen!' he said. 'The spook is saying "What?"'

'What?'
I said.
'Yes, "what".'
'What?'
'Yes, that's what it's saying.'

He wasn't making any sense.

'Come here, Damian,' he insisted. 'Listen again.'

Just to please him, I put my ear to the door. I was amazed. I could hear real words.

'What's going on?' said the voice.

It was no ghost, after all.

We pushed the chest out of the way and opened the door. There was the Major in a long white dressing gown with Mrs Harrington-Smythe standing next to him in a long white nightie.

Was it any wonder I had made a mistake? Who wouldn't have thought they were ghosts?

'We heard you scream,' the Major said. 'I expect you were worried when the lights went out.'

I shook my head. 'The dark doesn't frighten me. I stay cool.'

'Well, if you're sure . . .'

'Sure. Don't you worry about us,' I said. 'In fact, we can't wait to come face to face with the ghosts.'

The Major smiled. I think he felt reassured that we were on the job. Soon they would be saying adios amigos!* to all their problems.

Mrs Harrington-Smythe, who was carrying a candlestick, said, 'We're going to bed now, dears. The electricity should be back on in the morning. Good night.'

They turned and headed down the corridor and we shut the door.

'So there weren't any ghosts,' said Harry.

'No. You needn't have worried,' I said.

'I wasn't worried,' said Harry.

'What did I tell you?' I said. 'It pays to stay calm.'

---

*I am hoping to go on holiday to Spain and I am learning the lingo.

We agreed to take it in turns to keep watch through the night. Harry climbed into the bed and was soon snoring like an old goat.

I sat in an armchair, fully alert, with my notebook in my hand.

But, at exactly ten past eleven, IT HAPPENED.

The door knob turned. I sat bolt upright and fixed my eyes on the big oak door as it opened very, very slowly. The old hinges creaked. Spooky, spooky, spooky!

But was I scared?

No.

Did I panic?

No.

Did I yell?

No.

This time I was ready.

Chapter 7

First came the noise.

'Oooooooooo Oooooooooooooooooh.'

Then came a blast of cold air as a ghost slowly drifted through the open door and into the room. You should have seen it! It was white from head to toe, except for the black top hat. It was just like the man in the painting – beard and all. Without doubt, this was the murdering ancestor of Major Harrington-Smythe.

Of course, I wasn't frightened but I decided to hide under the bed.

This was so I could watch what was going on without being seen.

I didn't have long to wait before a second ghost came in. This one was white, too, but much smaller and wore a grey shawl. She was carrying a bundle which I guessed was a baby.

I was certain it was the ghost of the woman who had been murdered.

What happened next was horrifying. From my hiding place, I saw the man-ghost turn to the woman-ghost and grab her by the throat, making her scream. It was such a terrible scream that I had to cover my ears.

Aaaaaaaagggggggggghhhh!

I was about to leap out and strike him with some garlic when I felt the bedsprings over my head begin to shake. Harry had woken up. At first I thought he was trembling with fear –

but no. The bed was shaking because Harry was swinging on the crossbeam of the four-poster bed – just like Tarzan. He swung several time before and letting go and lunging at the man-ghost.

'Leave off her, you bully,' he yelled and kicked the murdering ghost in the belly.

The ghost yelled, 'Aaaaaaaaaagh!' and fell back, staggering towards the door and losing his top hat as he went. It was then that I knew this was no ghost. Under his hat was thick, dark hair. It was all a trick.

But the man-ghost didn't hang around. He was out of the room in a flash.

'Go after him, Harry,' I yelled from under the bed.

Unfortunately, the man-ghost ran down the corridor and climbed out through the landing window before Harry moved.

'Don't just stand there, Harry!' I yelled. 'Stop the other one!'

But the woman-ghost was clever. She flung her shawl over Harry's head, pushed him out of the way and ran out through the door.

'Tough luck,' I said, getting out from under the bed. 'Try to be quicker next time.'

Seconds later, there was the sound of breaking glass followed by a scream. The woman-ghost had slipped as she climbed out of the window and she'd fallen onto the greenhouse.

'Let's go, Harry,' I said. 'Follow me to the garden.'

All this noise had woken the Major and his wife who came staggering, half-asleep, out of the guest bedroom.

As we dashed passed, I yelled, 'Everything's under control,' but they followed behind, as fast as the Major's creaking knees would allow.

As we dashed out of the front door, I leapt over the pile of onions and garlic.

Harry leapt over them.

But the Major didn't see them and he

tripped over the onions and the garlic.

Then Mrs Harrington-Smythe tripped over the Major.

We didn't have time to help as we had a crime to solve.

Harry and I hurried across the lawn until we reached the vegetable patch. We were in luck! The woman-ghost was limping between the rows of runner beans. So I dashed forward and jumped in front of her, holding my wooden stake and garlic.

'I am Damian Drooth,' I said, 'and I am arresting you for . . .'

'What?' she said. 'You're just a kid.'

And she whacked me across the shoulder with the baby (which wasn't even real) and sent me spinning backwards into a prickly blackberry bush, taking Harry with me. It was very painful. By this time Annabelle's grandma was back on her feet. She bashed the ghost-woman over the head with a bunch of onions and sent her flying. So that was OK.

One ghost down. One to go.

'The man-ghost must be around somewhere,' I whispered to Harry as I tried to remove some very nasty thorns from my behind. 'He can't have got away.'

'What do we do, Damian?'

'I have a plan,' I said.

It was obvious to me that there must be a getaway car somewhere nearby. We walked out onto the street and I soon spotted it. It was a flashy red model parked near to the gate – the kind of car that makes a noise like a sports car but isn't. In my experience, this is the kind of car that crooks use.

'Watch and learn,' I said to Harry.

I sneaked up to the red car, bent down and let the air out of the front tyre, then the back tyre. But before I could finish, I saw the man-ghost jump over the wall of the Grange and come running along the pavement towards me.

'Hide,' I said to Harry and we stepped back into the shadows.

We watched as the man-ghost ran for the car. But he didn't go for the red one. He jumped in a tatty old green one instead.

Was that bad luck or what?

Chapter 8

I have to admit that, for once, our local police were brilliant.

As the man-ghost pulled away from the kerb, a police car, with lights flashing and siren blaring, came speeding down the road and skidded to a halt, blocking the road and stopping him going anywhere.

I dashed over to a police woman as she climbed out.

'Just in time,' I said. 'I am Damian Drooth, ace detective. I expect Inspector Crockitt has mentioned me.'

She gave me a funny look. 'I am PC Honey,' she said. 'Did you let down these tyres, young man'.*

I ignored her question. Instead, I stood in front of her and said, 'I have

*Apparently, a man living over the road was the owner of the red car. He saw me let down the tyres and rang the police.

information which will be useful to the case of the Gruesome Ghosts.' And I pointed to the man-ghost in the green car. 'It was him!'

'He let down the tyres?' she asked. But before I could explain, PC Honey marched over to speak to him. When he tried to escape, she realised he was up to no good.

Anyway, things moved fast after that. A car came haring down the road, followed by a white van. They both screeched to a halt behind the police car. I recognised them at once. It was Mum (in the van) and Harry's mum and dad (in the car).

'DAMIAN!' Mum shouted. She didn't look very happy and I wondered if her dinner party hadn't gone well.

I tried to tell her what was going on. You'd think she would be interested to hear how I had uncovered the ghost scam. But she wasn't.

'You lied to me,' she said. 'I was frantic when I found out you weren't at Harry's house. It was only thanks to Tod and Lavender that I knew where you were.'

I made a note to have a serious chat with Tod and his sister. Revealing information is mega serious.

Mum didn't calm down.

'Not only did you go off without telling me but you took food that I'd made for my dinner party.'

'Only a bit,' I said.

Mum was shouting.

Harry's mum and dad were shouting.

The owner of the rubbish sports car was jumping up and down and carrying on about his flat tyres.

The woman-ghost was shrieking at

the Major as he dragged her towards the police car.

The ghost-man was bawling at the police woman who was arresting him for being suspicious.

Then somebody living in Rigby Road dialled 999 to say that there was a riot going on. So three more police cars arrived with blue lights flashing and made the road look like a parking lot.

I was relieved to see that Inspector Crockitt was in one of them.

'Damian!' he said, as he stepped out of the lead car. 'Why am I not surprised that you are involved in this?'

I smiled and turned to PC Honey. 'See. I told you I was well known.' That showed her.

'You'd better come down to the station, Damian,' said Inspector Crockitt.

'Cool,' I said. 'I'm always willing to help the police.'

Chapter 9

Another triumph. The Case of the Gruesome Ghosts was headlines in the local paper. Everybody was shocked to learn that Mr Snell the local estate agent and his secretary Primrose Dobbs regularly switched off the electricity

at the Grange before breaking in dressed as ghosts.

They wanted to scare Annabelle's grandparents into selling their home so they could build loads of houses in the garden and make millions.

'It was obvious all along that the ghosts weren't real,' I explained to Annabelle on Monday morning.

'Were you scared, Damian?' she asked. She was obviously dead impressed.

'Nah,' I said. 'Some people might be really frightened sleeping in that spooky old place. It was no big deal for me.'

Harry snorted. 'If you weren't scared, why did you hide under the bed?' But I ignored him. He's got a lot to learn.

As usual, there was no pleasing my mum. She made me do loads of work round the house – vacuuming and dusting and that.

'You'll have to learn to behave responsibly,' she said. 'You took some of the food I had made specially and my dinner party was ruined. Not to mention the terrible mess in the kitchen.' And she couldn't resist moaning about the garden. 'What were you thinking of – digging up MY LEEKS?'

I didn't bother trying to explain.

At least Major and Mrs Harrington-Smythe were well pleased that I'd saved them from a pair of criminals. They invited me and Annabelle to tea. (Harry couldn't come as he'd failed his

maths test and had to stay in to do extra work.)

While Annabelle tucked into strawberry jam and scones, I entertained her by describing all the methods of detection I use. I mentioned several of the cases I had solved and explained my plan for catching her grandparents' ghosts, step by step. Just as I was about to list my theories on Criminal Types, she suddenly remembered something of vital importance – she had to clean out her guinea pig hutch.

I offered to go with her and carry on our conversation. But she just said, 'I don't think so, Damian. Thanks for the advice. You never know, I might even set up my own Detective School.'

Then she started to giggle.

I'll never understand girls.